THE
MAGIC
DETECTIVES

D0770053

with illustrations by the author

PROMETHEUS BOOKS

BUFFALO • NEW YORK

 Inquiries should be addressed to Prometheus Books, 700 East Amherst Street, Buffalo, New York 14215, 800-421-0351; in New York State, 716-837-2475.

Library of Congress Catalog Card No. 89-62787
ISBN 0-87975-547-4

Manufactured in the United States of America

Contents

Introduction

Are ghosts, flying saucers, and "Bigfoot" real? Can someone actually read another's thoughts, or bend metal using only the power of the mind? What are the secrets behind firewalking, mysterious disappearances, the "mummy's curse," and other strange phenomena?

Now you can discover the answers to such questions as you learn how to become a "magic detective." With the help of this book you can investigate strange mysteries and paranormal happenings—that is, things that seem beyond the range of nature and normal human experience.

Each of the thirty cases presented here contains clues to help you to unlock its secret. When you read about these mysteries, try not to work backward from what you think might be the answer. Instead, look for pieces of evidence that support one another, and try to let the evidence lead to a solution.

Also, strive to be skeptical—or doubtful—about things that don't seem to make sense. Keep in mind the principle that "extraordinary claims require extraordinary proof."

When you think you may have the answer to one of the

mysteries, read the solution and compare it with your own. Don't be discouraged if yours is different. You may have a valuable idea that is worth talking over with your science teacher. The important thing is to learn to think critically.

If you find you have a knack for solving these riddles, you may wish to research other mysteries that you read or hear about. The sources listed at the end of this book may prove helpful. Some, however, are technical, so ask your mom or dad, a teacher, or a librarian for help in selecting the right books and articles for you.

Someday, you may wish to join up with the magic detectives of CSICOP—the Committee for the Scientific Investigation of Claims of the Paranormal. This is an international organization that examines supposedly paranormal phenomena by using the scientific method and other tools of critical thinking, and publishes the results of its investigations in a journal called the *Skeptical Inquirer.* CSICOP was founded by the philosopher Paul Kurtz, the magician James "The Amazing" Randi, the writer Philip J. Klass, scientists like Carl Sagan and Isaac Asimov, and others.

In the meantime, brace yourself for some fascinating and often spine-tingling mysteries, and for some revealing and surprising solutions. Happy sleuthing!

1

Lady, the Wonder Horse

Lady Wonder, the so-called "talking horse," could read minds—or could she?

Lady was one of a long line of "educated" animals that includes pigs, dogs, and geese. In seventeenth-century France, for example, a famous "talking horse" named Morocco seemed to possess such remarkable powers that he was charged with "consorting with the Devil." However, he saved his own life and his master's when he knelt before church authorities, seemingly repentent.

Such animals answer specific questions posed by someone other than their trainers—who are always present when the animals perform. They "talk" by stamping a hoof (say, once for *yes* and twice for *no*) or by spelling out answers using alphabet and number cards.

Many of these animals are said to have extra-sensory perception (ESP), and to be able to read the minds of their questioners. Lady was one of these type of animals. She performed in a red barn near Richmond, Virginia, during the 1920s and 1930s, and used her nose to nudge out her answers letter by letter on a big typewriter-like device.

In this way, Lady could spell out a stranger's name—although it was supposedly unknown to her. Or she could indicate a number someone was merely *thinking* of. Lady certainly seemed to read minds!

But a magician named Milbourne Christopher was suspicious, and wanted to test the horse's ESP. He visited Lady, but was introduced to her trainer, Mrs. Claudia Fonda, as "John Banks." He knew that if Lady really did have ESP, she would know his real name, no matter what he told her trainer.

"What is my name?" Mr. Christopher asked the horse.

Lady lowered her head and pressed a lever so that the letter *B* popped up. Then followed the letters *A, N, K,* and *S.*

Mrs. Fonda then gave Mr. Christopher a pad of paper and a pencil. She asked him to write down a number, and to concentrate on it. She said that Lady would use her powers of ESP to learn what it was.

Mr. Christopher pretended to write a *9* but he actually wrote a *1.* Again, if Lady really had ESP, she would know the correct number. Lady nudged a lever and indicated the number *9.*

Mrs. Fonda, of course, had been watching Mr. Christopher,

and had thought he had written a *9*. Remember, she also had thought his name was Banks.

But how does this explain Lady's incorrect answers? Could it be that Lady was actually reading her *trainer's* mind? Or is there another possibility?

Solution

Lady had been trained to sway her head back and forth over the levers. Milbourne Christopher observed a "slight movement" of Mrs. Fonda's training rod when Lady reached the correct letter or number. That was enough to cue the horse to stop, and she nearly always got the "correct" answer this way.

Lady Wonder was indeed a clever horse, but she could read minds no better than any ordinary horse—that is, not at all!

2

The Ghost Girl

Do ghosts really exist? Are some "spirits of the dead" condemned to a lonely, earthbound existence—making their presence known to ordinary people from time to time?

Reports of ghostly occurrences have persisted since ancient times. Often, people hear strange noises or experience physical disturbances that they attribute to ghosts because they do not know the non-ghostly sources of these events. Less often are ghosts seen, and then usually by a single person, giving others cause for skepticism.

Take the case of the ghost girl. A well-known "ghostbuster," Dr. Robert A. Baker, professor of psychology at the University of Kentucky, was called in on this case by the young married couple whose home she visited. They wanted desperately to have a baby, but were unable to.

One day when the wife was at home alone, an apparition, or image, of a child appeared to her. The little girl was judged to be about four years old. She showed herself briefly, and then faded from view. She appeared several times after that, showing herself only to the wife. Although the girl never spoke or caused any disturbance, the husband and neighbors were concerned. The experience was somewhat unsettling, because it was out of the ordinary.

Dr. Baker never saw the ghost. He examined the house, and did not find any evidence of paranormal happenings. He then counseled the couple, offering a prescription for their troubles. They took his advice and it had a profound and beneficial effect on their lives, resulting in the ghost girl's vanishing into the realm from whence she came. Can you judge from the clues whether the ghost girl was real? Can you also guess what Dr. Baker recommended that the couple do?

Solution

Dr. Baker often says, “There are no haunted houses, only haunted minds.”

Note that the “ghost girl” appeared only to the childless woman who wanted very much to have her own little daughter. Dr. Baker saw this as evidence for his “haunted mind” theory, suspecting that the apparition was one of the woman’s imaginings and was borne of her own sadly unfulfilled wishes.

His prescription? He recommended that the couple adopt a child. They did, and the little “ghost girl” vanished forever.

3

Walking on Fire

Firewalking is an ancient Asian art that has mystified many people. It is often associated with a religious ritual, and firewalkers claim that it requires meditation or even mystical powers to accomplish. Certainly it seems remarkable that someone could walk barefoot across red-hot embers without so much as a blister. How is this possible?

Typically the walk is part of a lengthy and elaborate ceremony that begins with the preparation of the fire itself. During the ceremony the wood fire, which is usually set in a trench about a dozen feet long, is allowed to burn down until only a bed of glowing coals remains. (The fire may seem hotter than it really is, because the sides are usually heaped highest.) Then the mystic quickly performs the walk.

One theory to explain the phenomenon was that because firewalkers usually go barefoot, their feet became toughened. Another notion was that they used a special preparation on the soles of their feet to protect them from burning. However, these ideas are no longer believed to be the causes.

Years ago some interesting experiments were done with an Oriental firewalker. He was able to walk about twelve feet (a few quick steps) across a bed of coals that was 1130 degrees Fahrenheit. However, when the trench was extended to twenty feet long and the heat increased to 1460 degrees, he suffered burns.

Bernard Liekind, a physicist, has actually walked on fire. He insists that no magical power is involved. Instead, he says firewalking can be explained by natural laws. From what you have just read, do you believe Dr. Liekind is correct, or do you believe firewalking is due to some paranormal ability? What does the evidence suggest?

Solution

Dr. Liekind explains that several physical factors must be considered in understanding firewalking. First of all, wood does not conduct heat well. (In contrast, a person could not walk on *metal* heated to the same high temperatures as the coals, without being severely burned. That is because metal is a good conductor of heat.)

Other physical factors are involved, including the time of contact. Experiments have shown that people can manage a very short walk over high-temperature coals, or a longer walk over cooler coals. (Most people know they can draw a finger quickly through the flame of a candle. But if they pause or move too slowly, they will get burned.)

Ripley's "Believe It or Not" claimed one firewalker strode the length of a twenty-foot trench heated to 1400 degrees Fahrenheit. Actually the trench was divided at the middle by a crosswise section of dirt where the walker paused briefly. Thus his performance consisted of two short walks of ten feet each, not a single twenty-foot walk.

Although firewalking can be risky unless you know what you are doing, it requires no theory of mystical or magical forces to explain it.

4

The Tragic UFO Chase

On January 7, 1948, Air National Guard pilot Thomas F. Mantell died when his plane went down following an encounter with an Unidentified Flying Object (UFO).

During the previous year the term "flying saucers" had been coined by a newspaperman after an incident in Washington State. Since then there had been a rash of saucer reports.

Captain Mantell was the leader of four P-51 fighter planes on a low-altitude flight from Georgia. When they were in the vicinity of Godman Air Force Base, near Fort Knox, Kentucky, the base radioed a request that they investigate a UFO.

The strange object had been the subject of several reports made to the Kentucky State Police, and it was then sighted by tower operators at Godman. It appeared to be moving in a southwesterly direction. Soon the pilots had it in view.

It was described by observers as resembling a parachute or "an ice cream cone topped with red," as appearing "round like a tear drop . . . at times almost fluid," and as looking "metallic and of tremendous size." Two other unusual aerial objects were reported in the general area sometime after Mantell's encounter, one later than the other. They were miles to the southwest, and each was identified through a telescope as a balloon.

Mantell radioed, "I'm closing in now to take a good look. It's directly ahead of me and still moving at about half my speed. . . ."

His voice became a bit groggy as he said, "It's going up now and forward as fast as I am . . . that's 360 mph. I'm going up to 20,000 feet, and if I'm no closer, I'll abandon chase."

Mantell had decided to "abandon chase" at 20,000 feet because his plane was not oxygen-equipped and could not fly higher than that altitude because the atmosphere is too "thin."

One of the other planes tried to radio Mantell, but he failed to acknowledge its message.

Nothing further was learned of him until his wrecked plane was discovered. Speculation and rumors grew that he had been shot down by a spacecraft from another world. As an investigator, would you suggest a different possibility?

Solution

Air Force investigators concluded that Captain Mantell passed out from lack of oxygen after flying too high. Thus, his plane went into a spiral dive and crashed.

At the time, the U.S. Navy was using huge "Skyhook" balloons for cosmic-ray research, but since the government had kept their existence secret, investigators were baffled. Such balloons fit the descriptions of the cone-shaped object seen over Godman Air Force Base. A Skyhook can achieve high altitudes and, if caught in jet-stream winds, can reach speeds of more than 200 miles an hour. Or it can stop and seem to hover, or move erratically, or execute sharp turns, depending on the winds. It can even appear to change its shape and color. Depending on how sunlight strikes the plastic covering, the balloon can appear to be white, metallic, red, glowing, and so on.

So often have balloons of one type or another been reported as UFOs that, when lost, these chameleons of the sky have often been traced by following the reports of saucer sightings!

Eventually it was learned that a Skyhook balloon had been launched from Southern Ohio "on or about 7 January 1948," the date of the Mantell encounter. The two balloons that were sighted later and the object that Captain Mantell had died chasing were obviously one and the same Skyhook.

5

"Channeling" Spirits

"Channeling" is supposedly a method of communicating with spirits of the dead. Typically, the "channeler" appears to go into a trance, seeming to become a "channel" for the spirit's communication. That is, the spirit supposedly speaks through the channeler.

Originally known as "spiritualism," channeling began in 1848 with two young girls, Margaret and Katherine Fox; it soon became an international craze. They lived with their father, a Methodist minister, and their mother, a simple, superstitious woman, in a farmhouse at the village of Hydeville, New York.

One night strange knocking or rapping sounds began to be heard. These seemed to confirm the story that the house was haunted by the ghost of a murdered peddler. The raps appeared to center around the young girls, coming from their room although they seemed to be asleep.

Before long, the Fox sisters learned they could communicate with the ghost whom they named "Mr. Splitfoot." He responded to their questions by knocking a certain number of times to signal *yes, no,* or other simple answers.

"Mr. Splitfoot" followed the girls wherever they went. They even discovered they could communicate with other spirits, whether they were recently dead or had died a thousand years ago.

Soon, assisted by their older sister, the girls traveled all over the United States, promoting their "Spiritualist" society. They continued as "mediums" (as channelers were then called) off and on for the remainder of their lives. Meanwhile, many other mediums began to hold séances and to call up spirits.

On occasion the Fox sisters were challenged by scientific investigators. Some thought the rapping sounds came from under the table where Margaret sat. When the investigators controlled her feet, the sounds ceased.

Can you suggest why? What does the evidence say about the nature of the rapping phenomenon?

Solution

The Fox sisters were foxy. Margaret had a special knack of snapping her big toe against the bare floor to produce a rapping noise. (Her long dress hid her feet as she slipped off a shoe.)

Although this explanation strikes some people as farfetched, Margaret actually demonstrated her technique before a packed audience at a New York City music hall. And, as her sister Katherine nodded in agreement, she publicly branded spiritualism a fraud. (For the last six years of her life, however, needing money, Margaret returned to working as a medium. Thousands of believers came to her funeral in 1895.)

In his book, *The Psychic Mafia,* M. Lamar Keene explains how some modern-day spiritualists are still using tricks to convince people they are communicating with dead friends and relatives. Keene had himself been a phony medium at a spiritualist center. However, he reformed and wrote his book to help put a stop to the fraud.

Sitting in the dark, dishonest spiritualists sometimes cause "spirits" to appear. One way they do this is by waving about a piece of cloth that has been specially treated so that it glows in the dark. (With the use of cameras containing infrared film, magic detectives have often been able to obtain photos of such trickery.)

Sometimes, spiritualists conduct research on the people who will be attending their séances. The information they obtain is then given out during the medium's apparent "trance." That way, it looks as if the information was provided by spirits. As a result, gullible people often make large donations to spiritualist "ministers" and their "churches."

Many of today's channelers avoid out-and-out trickery. Typically, they just go into their "trances" and seemingly allow "spirits" to speak through them. Most of the supposed messages from the dead consist of little more than vague advice about "getting in touch with yourself," learning to use your "hidden powers," and other fuzzy sayings.

6

The Everywhere Panda

On December 10, 1978, a small panda escaped from the zoo in Rotterdam, a city in the Netherlands. Immediately zoo attendants informed the local newspaper which carried the story. People were urged to help find the panda.

Almost as soon as the paper hit the stands, panda sightings began to be reported all across the Netherlands. Over the next few days, many people phoned the zoo, claiming to have seen the lost panda. In all, some one hundred calls were received.

Obviously a single panda could not have traveled so fast and so far. And just as surely, there could not have been more than one of the rare animals on the loose. In fact, the panda was found just a few hours after it was discovered missing, at about the same time the newspaper reported its disappearance. It had only wandered about five-hundred yards from the zoo to a railroad track where, sadly, it had been struck and killed by a train.

But what about all those sightings? Had something paranormal occurred, or can you think of a more reasonable explanation?

(Before reading the solution, you may want to have fun by seeing if you can find all the pandas in the accompanying illustration.)

Solution

It is possible that some people saw dogs or foxes or other animals that they mistook for the missing panda. Others may have only *thought* they saw something. Still others who phoned in their sightings may have been pranksters.

In any case, the flurry of sightings represents what psychologists—experts who study the mind—call "contagion." Somewhat like a contagious disease, psychological contagion is transferable. That is, an idea, a custom, or an emotion can be spread from person to person until many become affected. This often appears to occur with reports of UFO sightings, hauntings, and the like.

(As to the pandas in the illustration, if you discovered all thirteen—including the shadow of one in the lower right-hand corner—congratulations!)

7

Tracking "Bigfoot"

Bigfoot is a big, hairy, ape-like "man-creature" of North American legend. It has been reported largely in the Pacific Northwest, but also in most other areas of the United States, including Ohio, Pennsylvania, and Florida.

Frequently, one Bigfoot sighting leads to an outbreak of "monster mania" (somewhat like what happened in the case of the "Everywhere Panda"). When that occurs, many people claim they have encountered one of the creatures.

However, not one Bigfoot has been captured or killed, nor

has a Bigfoot corpse or skeleton ever been discovered. There is a brief segment of poor-quality movie film that allegedly shows the strange beast running away from the camera, and there are a few other doubtful exhibits.

But for the most part the physical evidence for the creature consists of tracks left in the snow or mud. These often measure seventeen or more inches long—hence the name Bigfoot. The tracks have anywhere from two to six toes, and they vary considerably in their structure.

One group of Bigfoot tracks was discovered in 1930 near Mount St. Helens, Washington. Some people had gone into the woods to pick huckleberries, and when they returned to where their cars were parked, they found the huge footprints circling the area. They rushed to report them at the Ranger Station.

Two Forest Service workers who were present, however, knew the tracks were not those of the legendary Bigfoot, although they did not say so at the time. How might they have known the tracks were fake?

Solution

As indicated by the drawing at the beginning of this chapter, fake Bigfoot tracks are more common than authenticated ones; that is because there are *none* of the latter. Since no Bigfoot has ever been killed or captured so that its feet could be studied, no one knows exactly what kind of tracks the beast would leave if it did actually exist.

The film footage of "Bigfoot" is believed to be a hoax; researchers say that it is probably a movie of a tall man dressed in a furry costume.

As for the Mount St. Helens tracks, in 1982—more than fifty years after the incident—a retired logger confessed that he had helped to fake them. Rent Mullins, who had been working for the Forest Service in 1930, told how, as a prank, he had carved a pair of 9-inch-by-17-inch feet from a piece of wood. Then, a friend, Bill Lambert, attached them to his own feet and walked around the huckleberry pickers' automobiles. Mullins and Lambert were at the Forest Service office later when the excited pickers reported the tracks.

8

Dark Days

There have been several mysterious "dark days"; the most notable occurred in the eastern United States on May 19, 1780. It began with the approach of black clouds from the southwest, and it grew so dark over much of New England that a minister described it as having "the appearance of midnight at noonday." Schoolchildren were sent home, where their parents were forced to light candles, lanterns, and lamps in the middle of the afternoon.

Of course, the people did not have radios, and it would be

days before out-of-town newspapers and letters arrived, so they had no way of knowing how extensive the phenomenon was. People became terrified; many feared that doomsday had come, and they gathered in their churches to pray.

When a member of the Connecticut Legislature moved to adjourn, one of his colleagues replied: "Mr. Speaker, it is either the Day of Judgment, or it is not. If it is not, there is no cause for adjourning. If it is, I desire to be found doing my duty. I move that candles be brought and that we proceed to business."

Members of the animal world seemed less perturbed by the event, but they *were* fooled by the darkness. Reportedly, chickens went to roost, night birds set to whistling, and frogs began their familiar nighttime sounds.

A Massachusetts professor named Samuel Williams had the presence of mind to examine some of the rain that fell during the dark day. He described it as having "an uncommon appearance, being thick, dark, and sooty." This eighteenth-century sleuth went on to provide a key to the mystery.

What was the ominous phenomenon that had snatched the light from a New England spring day? Are there clues that tell you what may have darkened the sky?

Solution

Professor Williams examined a quantity of the "sooty" material from the rain and concluded that "in taste, color and smell, it very plainly appeared to be nothing more than . . . the black ashes of burnt leaves." The dark clouds that appeared to bring on the obscurity were obviously laden with soot and ashes. This material probably came from a great forest fire somewhere in the western frontier. In fact, for two days before May 19, the sky was said to have had a "smoky" aspect. This is the usual scientific explanation of other dark days as well.

9

The Haunted Stairs

The Canadian rebel-statesman William Lyon Mackenzie (1795–1861) lived a colorful and turbulent life. He died in his now-historic home—but continues to roam its corridors, according to two couples who have lived there as caretakers.

The story of the spooky shenanigans became known in 1960 when Mr. and Mrs. Alex Dobban, who had been living in the house for a little more than a month, told their story to the *Toronto Telegram* and attested to certain ghostly events, including mysterious footsteps on the stairs late at night.

Subsequently, Mr. and Mrs. Charles Edmunds, who had been the caretakers from 1956 to 1960, came forward with similar tales.

The narrow, three-story residence stands on Bond Street in downtown Toronto. Only forty inches away is the office (and warehouse) building of Macmillan and Company, the book-publishing firm. (See sketch.) Directly opposite the Mackenzie staircase is a parallel one at Macmillan. But a 1972 investigation showed that that building's staircase was not haunted, and Macmillan's late-night cleanup crew had never experienced anything unusual.

Shortly after the caretakers had moved out of Mackenzie House, two newspapermen spent an uneventful night there. Also, a clergyman conducted an exorcism (a religious ceremony to drive out demons), workers reported odd occurrences, and "psychics" and curiosity seekers were drawn to the alleged "haunted house." Widely reported during this time was the phenomenon of the ghostly footfalls.

As one of the caretakers, Mrs. Edmunds, had described them: "They were thumping footsteps like someone with heavy boots. This happened frequently when there was no one in the house but us, when we were sitting together upstairs."

Mrs. Dobban stated: "We hadn't been here long when I heard footsteps going up the stairs. I called to my husband, but he wasn't there. There was no one else in the house—but I definitely heard feet on the stairs."

Can you deduce the solution? Was old Mackenzie's ghost really treading upon the stairs, or was there another source for the phantom footsteps?

Solution

Investigations by the author in 1972 and 1973 revealed a variety of causes for the assorted phenomena. (The case is discussed fully in the author's *Secrets of the Supernatural,* 1988.)

To solve the case of the mysterious footsteps, recall that the staircase in the Macmillan building was *adjacent* to Mackenzie House, "only 40 inches away." Note also the presence of late-night workers who would, naturally, have used the stairs. In fact, the Macmillan staircase is made of iron, which amplifies the sound of footsteps. To the caretakers next door who were sitting or lying upstairs, quietly thinking of ghosts, the illusion of spirits treading the steps was a convincing one.

10

The "Two Will Wests"

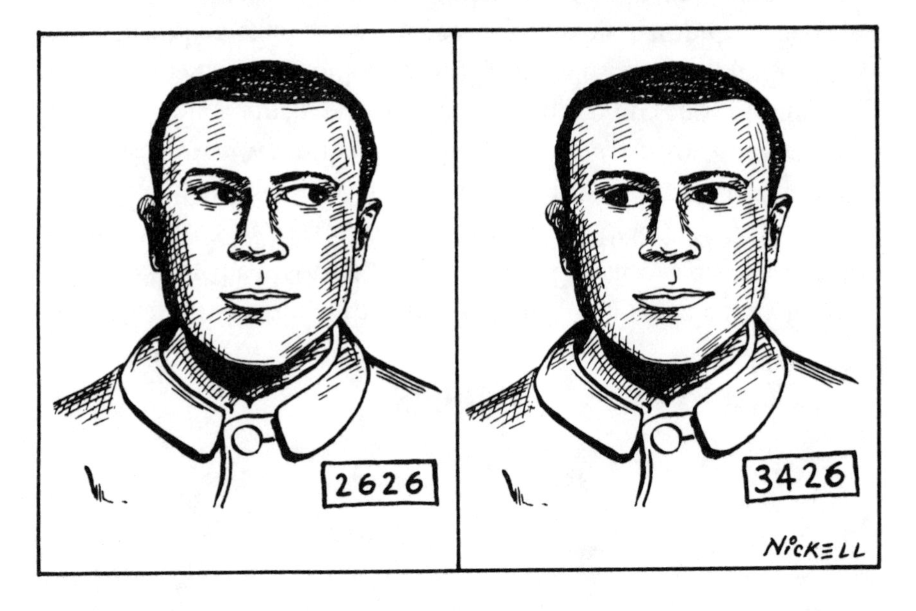

Astonishing coincidences happen. Sometimes events even seem to have an almost mystical relationship. Such was the unique case of the "two Will Wests."

The story, about "one of the strangest coincidences in all history," begins in 1903. At that time a young black man named Will West was admitted to Leavenworth Prison in Kansas to serve a term for manslaughter. The records clerk thought he recognized him, but Will West denied having been imprisoned before.

Soon, however, the clerk found the file on a "William West." Not only did the two individuals have similar names, but they also had almost identical measurements. (These were quite detailed, since measurements were then the primary means of identification.)

"That looks like me, all right," Will West conceded. But he continued to protest that it could *not* be him since he had no prior arrests.

At this point officials realized that—according to the records—William West was a "lifer," sentenced for murder and supposedly still within the prison walls. Had he been released by mistake? Worse, had he escaped? Or was he just pulling a stunt, pretending to be a new prisoner in order to avoid work for a while?

A check was immediately made, and in a short time the two men—William West and Will West—stood together in the same room. Incredibly, the men looked "identical," even as "alike as twin brothers." However, they denied being related, and at the time no one was able to prove otherwise.

Fortunately the new science of fingerprinting made it possible to distinguish one man from the other. Although the sets of patterns were similar, fingerprint experts could easily tell them apart. Thus, the West case helped prompt the use of fingerprints for identification in America.

However, the mystery of the uncanny similarities remained. In 1979 the author began an investigation into the matter, receiving assistance from the FBI and from experts in many fields. Still more "coincidences" turned up. For example, records showed that both men were the same age, both had been born in Texas, and both had moved to Oklahoma when they were twelve or thirteen.

What do you think the author's investigation determined? Were the similarities proof that some mystical force was at work? Or was there a simpler explanation, as the author had suspected?

Solution

Note that the Wests not only had detailed measurements, names, and backgrounds that were alike, but that their fingerprint patterns were also similar. Experts thought this indicated that the pair were so-called “identical” twins.

The similarities continued to multiply. The men’s ear patterns were studied and—like the ears of twins—were found to be almost identical.

Significantly, the statement of a fellow prisoner was discovered in the old files. He had sworn that he personally knew the two men to be “twin brothers.”

Finally, records of their correspondence while they were in prison revealed that they had written to the same brother, the same sisters, and the same Uncle George. Taken together, this evidence supported the theory that the Wests were twins.

Obviously the Wests knew this, so why had they pretended otherwise? One possibility is that, in their criminal activities, one twin provided the alibi for the other. Or maybe, like twins everywhere, they enjoyed playing a prank—this time on prison officials.

11

The Vanished Tanker

In early February 1963, the S.S. *Marine Sulphur Queen* was on a voyage from Texas to Virginia—one from which it would never return. It was approaching the fateful region called the "Devil's Triangle."

Also known as the Bermuda Triangle and the Triangle of Death, it is a vaguely defined area of the Atlantic Ocean extending between and around Bermuda, Puerto Rico, and the tip of Florida. It has achieved legendary status because within its borders countless ships and airplanes, and even two nuclear submarines, have disappeared. Among the "theories" offered to explain the phenomenon are those involving "time warps," reverse gravitational fields, kidnapping by UFOs, even witchcraft.

The *Marine Sulphur Queen,* a tanker laden with 15,260 tons of molten sulphur, left Beaumont, Texas, on February 2, 1963. It was last heard from two days later at 1:25 A.M., when it was approaching the Straits of Florida. On February 8, when the tanker was one day overdue at Norfolk, a sea and air search was launched. In following days the search was widened.

However, neither the 523-foot tanker nor its crew of thirty-nine men was ever seen again. Nothing was ever found of the vessel except for a piece of an oar and a few damaged items marked with its name. It had seemingly vanished.

What had happened to the *Marine Sulphur Queen?* What was the nature of the mystery that had swallowed up a huge tanker? Can you find a clue that could provide an answer?

Solution

One clue to the fate of the *Marine Sulphur Queen* lies in the wreckage, which proves the ship did not simply vanish as some articles and books imply. The debris included part of a name board bearing the letters "ARINE SULPH" between its shattered ends. The lack of any distress message from the vessel shows that whatever happened to it occurred suddenly.

The tanker had been plagued by fires, and was believed to have encountered rough weather. Structurally weak (due to modifications it had undergone), it may have broken in half. Or, considering its cargo of molten sulphur, it might have exploded. (In 1972 this happened to a similar vessel, which carried the explosive liquid benzene.)

Actually, the ship probably never even reached the Devil's Triangle. Many tragedies have been attributed to that zone that in fact occurred elsewhere. In any event, the U.S. Coast Guard states that "there is nothing mysterious about disappearances in this particular section of the ocean. Weather conditions, equipment failure, and human error, not something from the supernatural, are what have caused these tragedies."

12

The Visions of Nostradamus

Probably the most famous "seer" or "soothsayer" (predictor of the future) was Michel de Nostredame (1503–1566). Better known as Nostradamus, he was a French physician and astrologer who has been variously described as a scholar, a sorcerer, and a fraud.

Nostradamus's predictions, or prophesies, were written in poetry. Their vague, symbolic language meant that they could be interpreted in different ways in different times. (Nostradamus admitted they were written so that "they could not possibly be understood until they were interpreted after the event and by it.")

For example, consider this verse:

> An Emperor shall be born near Italy,
> Who shall cost the Empire most highly.
> They shall say, from those around him he gathers,
> That he is less a prince than a butcher.

The second line is open to various interpretations. And what is left merely refers to a ruthless ruler born "near Italy"—that is, virtually anywhere in Europe or along the Mediterranean.

Thus, the four-line verse (or *quatrain*) could seem to refer to Ferdinand II, the Holy Roman Emperor who ruled from 1619 to 1637. Or it could refer to Napoleon, the French conqueror of the late eighteenth and early nineteenth centuries. Today's popular interpretation is that it refers to Adolph Hitler, the German madman who brought on World War II. And there are many other interpretations.

According to some accounts, Nostradamus actually showed visions to Queen Catherine. This took place in a "special apartment" that had a throne for the queen to sit on. It was placed in such a way that she would be looking into a mirror that was tilted at an odd angle and framed by large curtains. In the mirror she saw people enacting what she was told were "future events." The scenes seemed surprisingly real, almost as if she were looking beyond the mirror to actors on a stage.

Some investigators have wondered: What was the purpose of the mirror, and why was it tilted? Was the queen really seeing people in a vision, or is there some other possibility?

Solution

Assuming the incidents actually took place—which is by no means certain—if Nostradamus could really bring forth visions, why would he need a mirror? And why a *tilted* mirror?

Perhaps you have heard that stage magicians sometimes use hidden mirrors in creating their illusions. More than a century ago, a French scientist (an expert in optics, the study of vision) explained how Nostradamus could have deceived the superstitious queen.

There would actually have been *two* mirrors—one of them hidden behind the drapery—arranged like the mirrors in a periscope. The hidden mirror would reflect a scene portrayed by actors in another room, which would then appear in the seemingly magic mirror into which the queen gazed.

13

The Holy Shroud

A fourteen-foot length of linen cloth kept in a Catholic cathedral in Turin, Italy, has long been the subject of controversy. Known as the Shroud of Turin, it bears the front and back images of a crucified man, complete with red stains resembling fresh blood. Many believe it is the burial cloth of Christ. Some have suggested that the image is miraculous—though others are convinced it is a fake.

The cloth first appeared about 1357 in a village in France, where it was exhibited—for a fee—to large crowds of the faithful.

The Gospels had not mentioned Jesus' shroud having his picture on it; also no historical record from the thirteen centuries following the crucifixion mentions the cloth, and a fourteenth-century bishop claimed that an artist had confessed to having "cunningly painted" the image. However, this and other evidence was gradually forgotten, and the shroud eventually became a revered relic.

When the image was first photographed in 1898, it was discovered that where there should have been shadows, there were light areas; its darks and lights were actually reversed, as if the shroud were a photo negative of Jesus. Believers in the shroud's genuineness have argued that this ruled out forgery because no artist in the Middle Ages could have produced a "photograph of Christ" before photography was conceived of.

Several investigators have proved that when a cloth is draped over a three-dimensional form—such as a body—and then stretched flat again, a seriously distorted image results. The picture on the shroud, however, lacks the wraparound distortions that would have resulted from enveloping a body. Also, at least one simple artistic technique *can* produce shroud-like "negative" images—and this technique could have been done during the Middle Ages.

There was also disagreement over the "scientific" tests that had been performed over the years. Shroud advocates claim to have proved the red "blood" stains to be genuine, whereas skeptical investigators cite evidence that they are not, including the reported presence of paint pigments on the image.

Finally, much to its credit, the Catholic church agreed to permit dating tests on the cloth. In 1988, small samples of the fabric were removed and sent to three independent laboratories. Each was asked to date the origin of the shroud using the carbon-

14 method. (This is a very complicated scientific test that measures a material's percentage of radioactive carbon-14, which decays over time at a certain, fixed rate.)

What do you think? Is it a scientific approach to start out by suggesting a miracle? Can you foresee the results of the latest tests based on the clues at hand?

Solution

Observe that the "blood" stains have remained red, unlike genuine blood that darkens with age. This is consistent with the presence of paint pigments (including vermilion, a type of red pigment), as well as with the reported forger's confession and the lack of prior historical record. This evidence—taken together with the image's lack of wraparound distortion and the fact that an artistic technique can produce the "negative photo" effect—demonstrates that the "shroud" is actually a fake.

But this was proved conclusively by the carbon-14 tests performed in 1988. By this means three independent laboratories determined that the cloth dated sometime between 1260 and 1390—about the time of the reported forger's confession!

14

The Geller Effect

If countless bent keys, spoons, and other metal objects are sufficient proof, Uri Geller has a special ability. He can apparently bend metal simply by looking at it.

Using only his mental powers, he also appears to read people's minds, move objects, start or stop clocks and watches, "see" while blindfolded, and perform other wonders. These strange powers are known as the "Geller effect."

Geller, a former magician from Israel, says he discovered his strange powers when he was a schoolboy. He recalls that earlier, when he was three or four years old, he had had a strange experience while playing in a garden. He was surrounded by a brilliant silver light and then he fell unconscious. Now it is said that Uri is guided by super-beings from a distant planet.

Geller has been tested by researchers called parapsychologists. (They study such alleged phenomena as mind reading.) Few believe that Geller is guided by super-beings. Those who think he is genuine feel that the "Geller effect" may be some special power that science just cannot yet explain. Other researchers think he may have some legitimate powers but that he resorts to trickery when these become weak. Still others—particularly stage magicians—believe that Geller is a complete fraud.

Geller refuses to perform before skeptical magicians, who can duplicate his apparent marvels using clever tricks. But he says that is because skeptics have a negative influence on his powers.

What do you think is the most likely explanation for the "Geller effect"? How would you support your point with the evidence?

Solution

This is an example of "corroborative evidence"—that is, pieces of evidence that corroborate (or support) each other. These include the fact that Geller is a former magician, that magicians can duplicate his effects by clever tricks, and that he refuses to perform when magicians are observing. Apparently he is afraid that they might discover his trickery. In fact, Geller has actually been caught cheating.

Magician James "The Amazing" Randi once observed Geller up close. Randi posed as an editor of *Time* magazine when Geller performed in the *Time* offices. He saw Geller using simple tricks to work his wonders.

For example, although he pretended to cover his eyes while a secretary made a simple drawing, Geller actually peeked. This enabled him to seem to read her mind and reproduce the drawing. Also, instead of bending a key "by concentration," as he pretended, Geller bent the key against a table when he thought no one was looking.

In his book, *The Magic of Uri Geller,* Randi tells how other observers have witnessed Geller doing tricks, and how a photographer captured him on film faking a photo experiment. Randi also tells how Geller's acquaintances in Israel, his former girlfriend, and others associated with him knew firsthand about his trickery, some even helping him with it. This is the obvious secret of the "Geller effect."

15

The Mummy's Curse

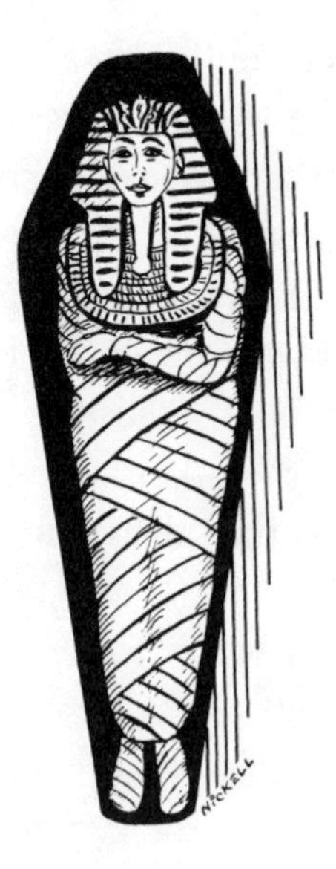

Many people believe in King Tut's curse—that, supposedly, death would come to anyone who disturbed the peace of that ancient Egyptian pharoah.

Tutankhamen (prounced Toot-ahnk-AH-men), or King Tut, ruled from the age of nine until his death at age eighteen, during the twelfth century B.C.

An archaeologist named Howard Carter—financed by a wealthy British nobleman, Lord Carnarvon—was making one last attempt to locate the lost tomb of the "boy king" when he discovered it in 1922 in the Valley of Kings, near Luxor.

Carter's workmen discovered first a step, then another and another—sixteen in all, leading to a sealed entrance. There was no inscription of any kind over this doorway, or indeed above any of the doorways leading to the inner burial chamber. Nor was there anything else to indicate whose tomb they had uncovered.

Carter waited for Carnarvon and his daughter to arrive from England. Then, having cleared away a rubble-filled corridor, the men found themselves at the entrance to the outermost chamber. Making a small hole, Carter inserted a candle and peered in.

"Can you see anything?" Lord Carnarvon asked anxiously.

"Yes," Carter replied. "Wonderful things."

The tomb was filled with treasures. Inside the actual burial chamber the men found the pharaoh's coffin. Actually, there were three coffins—one inside the other—the innermost of which was of solid gold. It contained the linen-wrapped, gold-mask-covered mummy of the boy king.

But not all was well. Even before the work was completed, Carter's pet canary was eaten by a desert snake. Then Lord Carnarvon died of blood poisoning from an infected insect bite. Carter ran into problems with the Egyptian government. In 1926 a woman who had formerly nursed Lord Carnarvon died in childbirth. One of Carter's assistants died in 1928 and another later. Over the years some archaeologists and tourists became ill or even died after they visited the tomb.

Newspapers blamed the events on the "curse." They reported that there was an inscription carved over the tomb's entrance that read, "Death shall come to him who touches the tomb." Some have suggested that a mysterious bacteria or fungus in the tomb causes people to become ill, but that does not explain their deaths.

Was a curse actually responsible?

Solution

As stated earlier, there was *no inscription*—curse or otherwise—above any of the doors leading to the pharaoh's mummy. Nor was any such curse found anywhere in Tutankhamen's tomb. In 1980 the tomb's former security officer admitted the story of the curse had been circulated in order to frighten away would-be grave robbers.

In any case, neither a curse nor mysterious bacteria would be needed to explain the deaths and other occurrences. Actually, a scientist took samples from the tomb only a day after the inner chamber was opened, and found only harmless bacteria. Anyway, remember that the so-called "victims" died of a variety of causes; some may have been ill anyway. The added effects of travel, climate, and other stressful factors may have contributed to any illness-related deaths.

Besides, if we were to focus on virtually *any* place—say a popular restaurant—we could expect similarly unfortunate events over the years: auto accidents nearby, illnesses and eventually deaths of those who once worked or ate there, and so on.

In fact, ten years after the pharaoh's tomb was opened, all but one of the five who first entered it were still living. Carter himself lived until 1939, dying at the age of sixty-six. Carnarvon's daughter and others associated with the tomb, including the photographer and Egypt's Chief Inspector of Antiquities, lived a normal life span. Dr. Douglas Derry—the man who actually dissected the mummy—lived to be over eighty years old!

16

The Amityville Horror

The most famous "haunted" house in America is located in Amityville, New York. Indeed, it has a gruesome history: There, in 1974, a man named Ronald DeFeo murdered his parents, brothers, and sisters in cold blood.

A year later, the house was bought by the Lutz family—George, Kathy, and their two boys. But they claim they were driven away after living there only twenty-eight days.

They said they had heard strange music. Green slime oozed from the ceiling. Kathy levitated (floated in the air) above her bed. Windows were damaged. The heavy front door was ripped off its hinges, and its doorknob was twisted. Outside the house, strange tracks were found in the snow—hoof tracks that some demon might have left, the Lutzes thought.

Reportedly, a priest who had blessed the house by sprinkling holy water in the different rooms heard a voice saying, "Get out!" He supposedly experienced other sinister phenomena. Police were reportedly called in to investigate.

These details were described in a best-selling book called *The Amityville Horror,* by Jay Anson, a scriptwriter who had worked on the movie, *The Exorcist.* A movie was later made that exaggerated the alleged events and even made up new ones like the frightening incident with the axe, shown in the accompanying drawing.

Investigators went to Amityville, soon after the book came out, checking out details of the story the Lutzes had told to Anson. The earliest newspaper article about the alleged events, which quoted George Lutz, made no mention of any damage to the house. Nor did it mention any levitation.

Neither local police officers nor the priest involved could provide much information. The priest said he had never been inside the house, and the police had never been called there to investigate.

Investigators also checked the weather reports for the dates in question. They found that on the date the strange tracks had supposedly been sighted outside the house, there had been no snow on the ground.

Does this mean that the case could not be solved? Match the facts the investigators learned with the alleged events George and Kathy Lutz described to Jay Anson. Is their account supported by the evidence? If not, what conclusions can you draw?

Solution

The fact that George Lutz did not originally mention any damage to the house suggests that none of the damage happened. Certainly no door had been ripped off its hinges. The hardware on the windows and doors had not been damaged or replaced, and no Amityville locksmith had been called by the Lutzes.

Similarly, because there had been no snow on the ground when George Lutz claimed to have seen tracks in the snow, that detail was false. Also untrue were the statements that police had investigated and that a priest had experienced various phenomena.

In fact, the story was a hoax. The lawyer of Ronald DeFeo—the man who had committed the murders in the house—had been planning to write a book. He later confessed that he and the Lutzes had "created this horror story over many bottles of wine." He added, "George was a con artist." Their motive had been money.

17

UFO Creatures

Ever since the "flying saucer" craze began in 1947, tales about encounters with saucer occupants have become common.

In the early years, the creatures were represented in various ways. Some were monsters of one description or another. Others were "humanoids" (human-like creatures) of differing sizes.

Eventually, the little humanoid type—like that featured in the movie *ET*—began to dominate the descriptions. ("ET" stands for *extra-terrestrial,* which means "beyond earth.") It was such a creature, reportedly, that was killed in 1953.

One night that year, three young men arrived at the offices of the Georgia newspaper, the *Atlanta Constitution.* They had with them the small body of a strange, man-like creature. It was non-human, but it was flesh and blood, resembling some type of primate. (Primates are highly developed mammals that include apes, monkeys, and man.)

The men claimed they had seen a red flying saucer parked in the road ahead of their speeding car. Three small creatures were scrambling to get into the spacecraft, but the vehicle slammed into one and killed it. The other two little humanoids made it safely into the craft, which began to turn blue and sped up and away.

Of course, the story caused a sensation—until reports came in that it was a hoax. Could the encounter have been a hoax?

Solution

According to Gene and Clare Gurney, authors of the book *Unidentified Flying Saucers,* the "humanoid" was a dead monkey; its tail had been cut off and its body shaved.

The hoaxer had done the work to win a ten-dollar bet, but a judge later fined him four times that amount for public mischief!

There have been many other fake encounters with extra-terrestrial beings. That is why, whenever such events are reported, they must be thoroughly investigated. Thus far, there is not enough proof to support any belief in such encounters.

18

Spirit Pictures

In 1985, about forty persons paid twenty dollars each to attend a séance. They sat in a darkened room, and their host, a "channeler," placed a small square of cloth in each of their laps. On these swatches, they were told, their individual "spirit guides" would draw self-portraits.

On a table at the séance was an open bottle of ink that would allegedly be used for the pictures. The channeler who was conducting the séance instructed the sitters not to turn the cloths over. He also urged them not to switch on the lights or even flick a cigarette lighter.

The channeler then went into an apparent trance, and soon "spirits" began to speak, delivering advice to the sitters. The "voices" were always male and a few people thought they sounded like the channeler's own voice!

Then, the channeler went around the room carrying a dim lamp with a red bulb which created an eerie effect. Each person turned over his or her square of cloth to reveal three or four "spirit" pictures that were about the size of fingerprints.

How do you think the pictures got there? Did they actually depict spirits?

99

Solution

Remember, the people in the room had not examined the swatches of cloth in advance; the channeler gave them the swatches and they did not see the other side of them until he instructed them to turn the cloths over.

There are no authentic spirit pictures for comparison. But an examination of the pictures was made by John F. Fischer, a forensic analyst. (He works in a crime laboratory where he is an expert in analyzing physical evidence.) His examination showed the pictures could not be distinguished from photographs, like those in magazines and newspapers. The ink had some of the qualities of printing ink that had been transferred to cloth.

The book *The Psychic Mafia* tells one way to make fake spirit pictures. A newspaper or magazine picture is soaked in ammonia, placed on the cloth, and pressed with a hot iron. (Experimentation shows that alcohol can be used instead, and the picture can be rubbed with a similar tool.)

The evidence indicates the pictures at the séance were prepared in this way. The persons attending the séance did not know this, of course. They assumed the cloths—which they held face down in the dark—were blank.

When Fischer examined the spirit pictures under special *laser* light, which reveals things that might otherwise be invisible, stains were observed around each of the small pictures. They had been caused by some liquid (such as alcohol) that had been applied in the area of each picture. This confirmed the other evidence that the pictures were transfers and, therefore, fake.

19

Photographing Fairies

The story begins in the village of Cottingly, England, in 1917. Two schoolgirls—Elsie Wright, age thirteen, and her cousin, Frances Griffiths, ten—said they encountered some fairies while playing in the woods. Since Elsie was employed in a photography shop, the girls happened to have a camera with them. They took a pair of photographs. One was of Frances with a group of dancing fairies and one was of Elsie with a gnome. The figures were so accurate in their detail that they were almost identical to those in children's books of the time.

In 1920, the girls took three more photos of the wee creatures. Careful examination apparently disproved any doubts about the photos' authenticity. A photographic expert stated that the pictures were not double exposures, nor were the prints or negatives tampered with in any way.

Sir Arthur Conan Doyle—creator of the famed storybook detective, Sherlock Holmes—was convinced. He wrote a book endorsing the genuineness of the photographs which brought them much public notice. Doyle did not believe that innocent children were capable of sophisticated photographic trickery, or that they would lie or have any motive to create a hoax. They even seemed eager to play down the affair.

For example, a reporter had to coax Elsie for an interview. She finally agreed but stated she was "fed up with the thing." He asked her, "Did you see [the fairies] come?" Yes, Elsie said, but when she was asked *where* they came from she said, laughing, "I can't say." Nor would she say where the tiny figures went after they had appeared for the camera. When he pressed her for an answer, the girl became embarrassed.

For some sixty years, the photographs were the subject of controversy. Skeptics thought the pictures were too good to be true, but believers defended the aging Elsie and Frances, who continued to protest their innocence. And then, suddenly, the matter was settled. Can you guess the outcome? What helped you form your opinion?

Solution

No doubt you noticed Elsie's evasiveness when she was being interviewed by the reporter.

Further grounds for suspicion came from the similarity of the fairies to those portrayed in children's books of the day. In fact, the "fairies" were merely cutouts made from those imaginary depictions.

By simply placing the cutouts in the scene and then photographing it, the pictures required no photographic trickery.

We know this because Elsie and Frances finally confessed to what began as a schoolgirls' prank but got out of hand when reporters and famous writers like Sir Arthur Conan Doyle became involved.

20

The UFO Explosion

Imagine a spaceship approaching earth from a far distant planet. On board, a malfunction develops. As an emergency landing is attempted, the saucer's nuclear power source detonates.

Is this science fiction? Or is it the true explanation for the "Tunguska [tun-GUS-kuh] event"? What is known for certain is that on the morning of June 30, 1908, a massive explosion occurred over the Tunguska River area of Siberia, in Russia.

The force of the explosion was equal to that of a hydrogen bomb. Trees were flattened throughout a circular area many miles in diameter. Small villages were destroyed. Hundreds of miles away, a great "pillar of fire" shot into the air, and smoke clouds rose several miles high.

Eyewitnesses had seen the UFO approaching earth on a collision course. Some described it as a cylinder-shaped object, but more saw it as a shining ball with a fiery tail.

Some flying-saucer theorists argue that radioactivity detected at the site proves the object was nuclear-powered. Skeptical scientists, however, say that the amount of radioactivity measured there is relatively small, and could have been produced by a natural event.

Can you guess what the natural event might have been?

Solution

The most common description provided by eyewitnesses—that of a spherical (ball-shaped) object with a flaming tail—matches that of a meteor. But a meteor should have left a crater, and some UFO theorists insist that none was found.

Actually a group of craters was located at the site, in keeping with the explanation that a meteor exploded before impact. Soil analysis also supported the meteor theory.

21

The Early American Demon

Do "demons" sometimes inhabit a home, causing actual physical disturbances? According to the Puritan clergyman, Increase Mather (1639–1723), that is what happened in a New England home in 1679.

The home, in Newbury, Massachusetts, belonged to a man named William Morse, who lived with his wife and a grandson. The disturbances, which Mather thought were works of a demon or possibly the Devil, seemed to center around the boy, John Stiles.

The youth would sometimes suffer violent fits, shaking or jumping up and down. On occasion he would bark like a dog or cluck like a hen. At other times, his tongue would hang out. One writer has suggested the behavior might have been due to epileptic seizures. Epilepsy is a disorder of the nervous system that can cause convulsions or "fits."

But epilepsy cannot explain the other phenomena that occurred in the Morse home. For example, ashes were put into the family's food, an iron hammer was thrown at the grandfather, and objects—such as a chest—were moved from their resting places. As the elderly couple and the young boy lay at night in the same big bed, they would often be jabbed with sharp objects. Once, upon searching the bed, they found an awl, and another time they discovered a knitting needle, a large pin, and two sharp sticks.

Interestingly, the phenomena ceased whenever the boy was taken to a neighbor's house. But the disturbances would begin again when he returned home.

Then, a visiting seaman told the grandfather that if he could have the boy for a single day, he would put an end to the troubles. The man agreed, and the sailor kept his promise. There is no record of what he did or said, but the devilish acts ended.

Today, some researchers believe that disturbances like those in the Morse house are caused by *poltergeists*. That is a German word meaning "noisy spirits." Poltergeists have been blamed for setting fires, pelting people with stones, breaking dishes, overturning furniture, and causing similar mischief. Poltergeist activity almost always centers around an adolescent; when the child leaves, the activity ceases.

Because the youngster involved is often one who is disturbed about some family-related matter, some researchers have speculated that the activity might actually be psychokinetic—that is, that the unhappy "energy" surrounding the youngster might actually cause objects to move.

But skeptical investigators have found a much more common, everyday cause. Can you guess what it is?

Solution

Skeptical investigators have often discovered that a "poltergeist" was actually a child playing pranks. For example, the mystery behind several fires that plagued an Alabama house was solved by the confession of the family's nine-year-old son. He'd had a simple motive: He wanted his family to return to the city from which they had recently moved.

In another case—in a Louisville, Kentucky, home—boxes, bottle caps, and other objects were hurled about. Eventually an eleven-year-old girl admitted she was responsible for the trouble. Her mother was away, in a hospital, and the girl had wanted people to pay more attention to her. But she said: "I didn't throw all those things. People just imagined some of them."

The disturbances in the Morse house are most easily explained by the theory that the young boy caused them. He could have moved the objects, thrown the hammer, placed ashes in the food, and pricked his grandparents with sharp objects. *He* had probably hidden the objects that were found in the bed.

Pretending to go into a "fit," barking like a dog, and so on, would be very easy to do as well.

The fact that the phenomena did not continue when the boy was away from home and that it ceased completely after the sailor had a talk with the youth provides convincing evidence that the boy was responsible. No doubt the seaman made it clear he was not fooled by the childish pranks. He probably convinced the lad that it was wrong to cause such trouble.

Why had the boy misbehaved? The fact that he was living

with his grandparents, rather than his parents, could indicate that his family life had been disrupted, and he was unhappy about it. Perhaps, like the case of the little Alabama boy who wanted his parents to move back to the city, he was hoping to change his situation somehow. But becoming a little "devil" was the wrong way to go about it!

22

"Thoughtography"

Ted Serios claimed that he could merely *think* of pictures and cause them to appear on photographic film. The resulting images were called "thoughtographs."

These did not always turn out as desired, though. For example, Serios was asked to produce a picture of a sunken nuclear submarine, the *Thresher*. But the resulting picture looked like Queen Elizabeth II! Nevertheless, the fact that Serios could produce such pictures at all created a sensation during the 1960s.

All Serios did, apparently, to produce his thought-photos,

was look through a paper tube that he pressed against a camera lens. He used a Polaroid camera, which yielded the developed pictures in a few moments. This prevented film from being switched. In fact, Serios did not even handle the camera.

However, some magicians and photo experts were suspicious. They thought Serios might be slipping a tiny "projector" into the paper tube and then slipping it out again when the tube was handed out for inspection. Soon, they were able to duplicate Serios's feat.

Eventually, *Popular Photography* magazine challenged Serios to a sort of showdown. At first he did not wish to be tested by a team of photographic and sleight-of-hand experts. And when he did appear, he became unable to produce his amazing thought-pictures. Try as he would, the film remained blank.

At one point, a magician asked to examine the paper tube, to see if there was anything in it. Serios backed away, putting his hand in his pocket. However, no "thoughtograph" appeared, and the session ended with accusations on both sides.

The committee members suggested Serios was a fake, afraid to try his tricks before those who could detect them. On the other hand, Serios and his associate blamed the poor results on the hostile atmosphere. Which view do you think is most likely correct, based on the evidence?

Solution

Since there is no scientific proof that "thoughtography" actually exists, and since its effects can be duplicated by trickery, the photographers and magicians were right to be suspicious of Ted Serios.

His failure to produce results under test conditions seems to confirm the view that he was using trickery. So do his actions: Why did he back away and place his hand in his pocket? If he had nothing to hide, why did he mind being searched?

Serios's "projector" was never examined, but the skeptics used a small tube with a tiny magnifying lens at one end. At the other end was mounted a piece cut from a "slide" photo (a photo transparency used in a slide projector). With light shining over their shoulders (as Serios was always careful to have), the image was projected into the camera and onto its film.

23

Ancient Astronauts

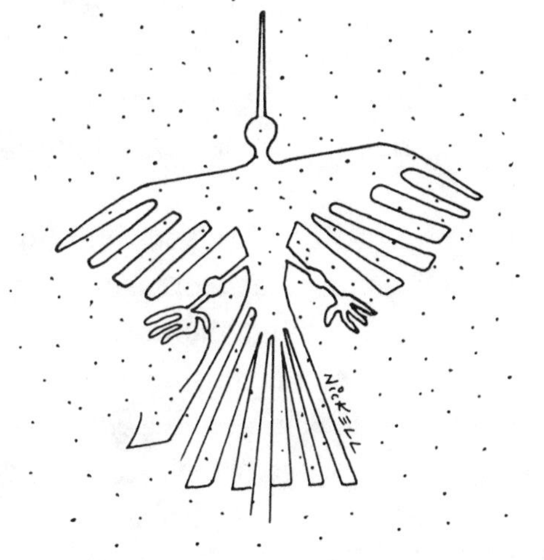

Called "Riddles in the Sand," great criss-crossing lines and giant drawings are marked across thirty miles of soft ground in the desert of southern Peru. The figures are of animals, birds, and other creatures, and are so large that they can scarcely be recognized except from the air. For example, the giant "condor," sketched here, measures 440 feet long—that is the size of more than one and a half football fields! The question is: Who made them and why?

In his best-selling book, *Chariots of the Gods?,* Erich von

Däniken argues that ancient visitors from a distant planet visited Earth and helped humans to built these large works and others, including the great pyramids of Egypt.

Von Däniken believes that the giant figures in Peru formed "signals" and "landing strips" for the flying saucers of these ancient astronauts. He thinks the "ETs" hovered over the desert and beamed down instructions for the markings to the native Nazca Indians.

The figures resemble those found on Nazca Indian pottery, and date from the time of the Nazca culture. Some people believe that they could have had some religious or ceremonial purpose that was central to the Indian lifestyle, although it is now puzzling to us.

Supposedly supporting Von Däniken's notions is the great size of the drawings. He claims that there is no way the primitive Indians could have made such huge pictures, which can only be identified from high above the Earth. But smaller, simpler drawings are found on hillsides in the area. Is it possible the Indians first made those drawings, which *can* be viewed from the ground, and then applied the same technique to the larger figures? Or do you agree with Von Däniken that flying saucers were involved? What do you think and why?

Solution

Von Däniken's ideas have been refuted by scientists and scholars. Having served prison terms for fraud of one kind or another, he has even been accused of distorting or falsifying some of his evidence.

In any case, as far as the Nazca drawings are concerned, evidence of extra-terrestrial visits is missing. As one expert noted, if flying saucers had attempted to land on the soft desert earth, they would have gotten stuck.

In 1982 the author and five assistants showed it was possible to reproduce the giant Nazca figures using only simple materials such as the Indians might have used. With just sticks and knotted cord, a giant "condor" was measured off, marked (like the lines on a playing field), and photographed from an airplane. According to *Scientific American* magazine, "The match with the Nazca original was remarkable in its exactness."

24

The Vanishing Olivers

In his book *Strangest of All* (1962), the writer Frank Edwards asks: "Is it possible for a human being to walk off the earth? Science says that it is not, but if that is correct, then what happened to Oliver Larch?"

According to Edwards, the Larch family farmhouse stood near South Bend, Indiana. Late on Christmas Eve, 1889, eleven-year-old Oliver was sent to fetch water. But no sooner had the boy started toward the well than he was heard crying for help.

His parents and some visitors rushed outside, but Oliver's

cries were already growing fainter. Reportedly the witnesses later agreed that the cries had seemed to come from the darkness overhead! By lamplight all that could be seen were Oliver's tracks, which ended abruptly. According to Edwards, "There were no other marks of any kind in the soft snow. Just Oliver's footprints . . . and the bucket . . . and silence."

Eventually, investigators attempted, unsuccessfully, to check out details of the story. They wanted to learn whether there had been such an incident or even such a family. Instead, they discovered *another* Oliver who had vanished. His name was similar—Oliver Lerch—but he had supposedly been twenty years old and the event allegedly took place a year later, in 1890. He, too, had disappeared on his way to the well, his cries had seemed to come from above, and his tracks ended abruptly midway to the well.

But wait! Maybe the lad's name was really Oliver *Thomas,* the place a village on the island of Wales, and the date 1909. Again there were the same story elements: the strange cries and the abruptly ending tracks. Was someone or something—flying saucers, perhaps—kidnapping Olivers?

As it happens, a very similar tale had been told by Ambrose Bierce, the American short-story writer. Bierce's fictional account did not feature an Oliver, however. His character was a lad named Charles Ashmore. Charles had gone to a spring for water but had not returned. By the light of a lantern his father and sister saw that "the trail of the young man had abruptly ended, and all beyond was smooth, unbroken snow." Later, Charles's voice was heard, as from a "great distance."

As far as is known, Bierce wrote his story before any of the Oliver tales were published. Had fiction anticipated fact? If not, why were the tales so similar? What is the simplest explanation?

Solution

One clue is that investigators were unsuccessful in attempting to check out the Oliver Larch story. In fact, none of the tales checked out. There were no such people and no such events—the stories had no basis in fact whatever.

Another clue is that a very similar story—a fictional one—was published earlier. Ambrose Bierce's tale, one of three he wrote about "Mysterious Disappearances," no doubt served as a basis for the other stories.

Possibly, one writer "borrowed" Bierce's basic plot (changing the character's name and other minor details) and passed it off as a "true" account. Later, other writers did the same, borrowing from the borrower. Each of these minor writers made a few changes, but they lacked the imagination to invent a plot as intriguing as Bierce's original.

25

Bridey Murphy Lives Again

Can a person who has died actually live again, years later, in another person's body? In other words, is *reincarnation* (that is, being literally born again) a reality? If not, how do we explain the strange case of Bridey Murphy?

The story began in 1952 with an amateur hypnotist and a Wisconsin housewife named Virginia Tighe. The hypnotist supposedly "regressed" the woman. (That is, he took her back in time, mentally.) Under hypnosis, they claimed, Virginia "remembered" her earlier incarnation (or life) in nineteenth-century Ireland.

Speaking in an Irish brogue, Virginia described her prior existence as a red-headed Irish lass named Bridey Murphy. She gave accurate details about Irish life, although Virginia had never been to Ireland. At one session, just as she was coming out of her hypnotic trance, Virginia—or was it Bridey?—even danced an Irish jig.

Of course there were skeptics who looked into Bridey's story. While some facts checked out, others did not. A lack of records from the time and place of Bridey's life prevented the confirmation of the dates of her birth, marriage, and death. Also, some information "Bridey" had given was simply incorrect, and some important events that she should have recalled were unknown to her.

A newspaper pointed out that there were similarities between the lives of "Bridey" and Virginia. For instance, both had a mother named Kathleen, a brother who had died young, a childhood friend named Kevin, and so on. Virginia had once dyed her hair red—the color of Bridey's hair. Many people began to think that Virginia was only imagining having been Bridey. But how could she had learned about things long ago and far away?

Solution

It was true that Virginia had never been to Ireland, but she did have many connections with Irish ways throughout her life.

An uncle recalled how, as a child, Virginia had learned to dance jigs. A teacher remembered her participation in school performances, in which she had practiced speaking in an Irish brogue.

Perhaps she even read books about Ireland. In any case, "Virginia had a good imagination," said one of her girlhood friends. Apparently "Bridey" was a product of that imagination.

Reporters learned another striking fact: When Mrs. Tighe lived in Chicago as a child, an Irish family named Corkell lived across the street. It was reported (although apparently not proved) that Mrs. Corkell's maiden name was Murphy. In any case, her first name (spelled slightly different from that of her namesake) was *Bridie!*

26

The Loch Ness Monster

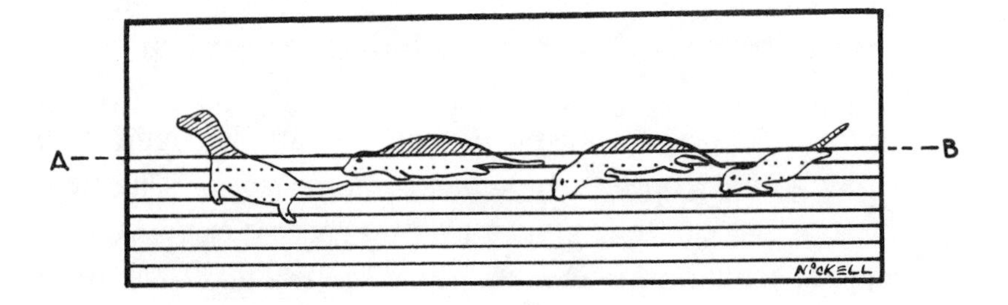

Reports of "sea serpents" are quite ancient. But does such a creature inhabit a great lake in Scotland called Loch Ness? Many eyewitnesses say so, the earliest report being from the sixth century.

The "monster" has been described in various ways. Reports of its length have ranged from 6 to 125 feet. At times the creature has resembled a giant eel but at other times it has had a large hump—or several humps (nine, by one count).

It has also had flippers, fins, a mane like a horse's, horns, tusks, and other various features. Then again, it has lacked those features. As if it were a chameleon (a small lizard able to change color) it has been described as silver or gray, brown, blue-black, black, and so on.

A popular theory is that the monster is a sea creature that somehow got into the twenty-two-mile-long lake. Possibly, they say, it swam up the River Ness, which links the loch to the sea. Some think that "Nessie," as the monster has been affectionately dubbed, may be a Plesiosaurus, a creature from the time of the dinosaurs. But scientists say that these became extinct millions of years ago.

Some sightings—and photographs—are known to have been hoaxes. Others have been blamed on misinterpretations of natural phenomena (for example, mistaking a floating log for the monster). Still others have been attributed to some animal such as a seal or a salmon.

One eyewitness thought he saw the monster but then decided he had seen a line of sea otters. Since otters are not common to the loch, the "creature" may actually have been a group of fish. (Cover the lower portion of the accompanying drawing—below line AB—to see one way a person could be fooled by something he saw.)

But what about actual physical traces? What about the large tracks that have been discovered along the shore of the loch? Zoologists (scientists who study animals) said they were exactly like the tracks of a hippopotamus. But hippos don't live along the loch, and none had escaped from a zoo. Can you offer a possible theory?

Solution

The tracks were fake. A hoaxer had produced them by using a cast made from a hippopotamus's hoof!

No genuine track or other certain trace of the "monster"—no carcass or skeleton, for example—has ever been found.

Time magazine once reported, "There is hardly enough food in the loch to support such leviathans [monsters]." The article added that "in any case, there would have to be at least twenty animals in a breeding herd [for the species to have continued to reproduce over the years]."

27

The Reverend Peter Popoff, Healer

The Reverend Peter Popoff is a faith healer—a person who claims to direct God's power to cure people of their illnesses.

Thousands of sick people go to his "crusades," or meetings, to be healed by Popoff. He appears to receive information about people and their illnesses by some secret means. He says that the information comes from God speaking to him. He may ask his audience, "Who is John? Is it John Smith?"

After John Smith identifies himself, he may be told something about a family member or about his home—some detail that Popoff supposedly would not know unless he was receiving a divine revelation.

Then the reverend will describe John Smith's illness and claim he will be healed. John Smith, of course, is very happy about this and believes that he has been touched by the hand of God. Many people do seem to feel better—at least for a time—and they often make large cash donations to the "crusade."

Interestingly, the people who go to see Popoff are asked to fill out information cards before the "healing" service. Whenever skeptics have deliberately given false information on their cards, it has been that *same* false information that Popoff later claimed God revealed to him.

Yet the preacher does not have the cards with him to read from, and he does not seem to have memorized the information.

Magician James "the Amazing" Randi learned that Popoff wears a hearing aid. Why could he heal others but be unable to cure his own apparent hearing problem?

Randi soon discovered the hearing aid was the secret to Popoff's ability to know facts about people. Can you explain how this might have been possible?

Solution

Actually, the "hearing aid" was a tiny radio receiver. Backstage, Mrs. Elizabeth Popoff would broadcast secret messages to him, reading the information that had been written on the cards or that had been obtained by interviews or other means.

But how were people cured? Some may have had illnesses that simply cleared up over time. Others probably just thought they were getting better, responding favorably to Popoff's positive suggestions. And in some cases, Popoff misrepresented the facts to make it seem that a miracle had occurred.

28

The Cinder Woman Mystery

Among the most gruesome of paranormal mysteries are those attributed to "spontaneous human combustion" (SHC). This is the supposed ability of human bodies to suddenly and mysteriously ignite, burning without any external source for the ignition.

Over the past three centuries, several unusual burning deaths have been blamed on SHC. What has become known as *the* case of SHC is the 1951 death of Mary Reeser. She was a widow who lived alone in a tiny apartment in St. Petersburg, Florida.

When last seen, the night before her remains were discovered, Mrs. Reeser was wearing a housecoat, sitting in a big stuffed chair, and smoking a cigarette. She told her son, who was a doctor, that she had taken two sleeping pills, and that she planned to take two more before going to bed.

The next morning, firemen called to the apartment extinguished a burning ceiling beam. There appeared to be little other damage to the apartment. Then they discovered Reeser's remains. Her body was so badly destroyed, along with the chair, that it was as if she had been cremated.

The carpet beneath the chair had burned through to the cement floor. The upper portion of the concrete-block walls were stained with smoke. A nearby lamp and end table had burned. Little else seemed to have been touched by the fire.

Those who believe in SHC have asked: How could Reeser's body have caught fire and been burned so severely, when the surrounding damage was limited?

Do you think SHC applies in the case of "the cinder woman"? Can you suggest another possibility?

Solution

There is no scientific basis for SHC. And in most of the purported cases there have been obvious causes for the fires: a broken oil lamp, for instance, or a knocked-over candlestick.

Obviously Reeser dozed off due to the sleeping pills, and dropped her cigarette. The big stuffed chair under her body supplied fuel for the fire that resulted, and because she was quite overweight (see drawing), her own body fat probably aided the burning.

The destruction of the apartment was limited because the firemen extinguished the spreading fire (the burning beam). Also note that the floor and walls of the apartment were made of concrete! That meant they could not burn.

Cases like this one are not very pleasant to think about, but they do happen. At least, they can remind us to be more careful with fire.

29

The Idol of Bel

One of the legends relating to the Old Testament prophet Daniel tells of his encounter with Babylonian priests and how he discovered the secret of the idol of Bel. (This is recorded in chapter fourteen of the Book of Daniel in the Revised Standard Version Common Bible.)

The events took place during the reign of Cyrus, the Persian King. The Babylonians had persuaded Cyrus to worship Bel. They had set up an idol, or statue, of Bel in the temple. Every day the Babylonians placed before the idol twelve bushels of flour, forty sheep, and fifty gallons of wine. The temple doors would then be closed, and by morning the entire meal would have been devoured.

Daniel was very wise and advised King Cyrus in many matters. Therefore, when the king demanded to know why Daniel refused to worship the Babylonian diety, Daniel replied that he believed in a *living* God.

Cyrus asked, "Do you not think that Bel is a living God? Do you not see how much he eats and drinks every day?"

But Daniel laughed, and said: "Do not be deceived, O King; for this is but clay inside and brass outside, and it never ate or drank anything."

At this, King Cyrus grew angry, as people often do when their beliefs are challenged. He summoned the priests of Bel and proposed a test between Daniel and the group of seventy priests. The loser—or losers—would be put to death. Cyrus arranged to have the food and wine set forth as usual, but to seal the door to the temple so that no one could enter without revealing the fact.

The following morning the seals were unbroken, yet the food was gone. But Daniel had taken extra precautions, setting a trap that revealed the priest's trickery. King Cyrus was convinced. He disposed of the priests because of their wickedness and allowed Daniel to destroy Bel and its temple.

Can you guess how Daniel uncovered the secret of the hungry idol? What would you have done in his place?

Solution

According to the legend, Daniel had instructed his servants to cover the floor of the temple with ashes. When morning came and the door was opened, Daniel restrained the King from entering, saying, "Look at the floor, and notice whose footsteps these are." Cyrus replied, "I see the footsteps of men and women and children." Then the priests confessed, and revealed the secret doors through which they and their families had been accustomed to enter. With such deceit had they partaken of the daily feast.

This story no doubt helped to motivate the Jews to resist idolatry. It can also be appreciated as a model of critical thinking—what the *New Catholic Encyclopedia* calls "clever detective work" from ancient times.

30

The Homing Coffin

The story of Charles Coghlan's coffin is one of the most incredible in the annals of the strange. It raises the question, Could the body of a man who died develop a "homing instinct"? Could it direct its coffin over ocean waters to a place many hundreds of miles distant—back to the land of his heart's desire?

Charles Francis Coghlan (1841–1899) was an actor born to Irish parents in Paris, France. He performed on stage in London and New York and, like many Broadway actors, spent his summers at Bay Fortune on Prince Edward Island, Canada.

The earliest—and shortest—published version of the returning coffin story is that of fellow actor Sir Johnston Forbes-Robertson, in his book *A Play Under Three Reigns.* Robertson says that Coghlan died at Galveston, Texas, adding, "Shortly after his burial there was a great storm come [sic] up from the Gulf which swept his coffin, with others, into the sea. The Gulf Stream bore him around Florida, up the coast, about 1,500 miles to Prince Edward Island and he came ashore not far from his home."

But no one was ever able to find the reburied coffin. Coghlan's daughter asked Forbes-Robertson if he knew where it was. Unfortunately, he was vague about how he had known of the story. And Coghlan's former manager could only say he had heard it "many times."

The story was related many more times, notably by Frank Edwards. He featured it in his 1964 book *Strange World.* And as it was told and retold, the story gained many specific details.

Coughlan's coffin had taken eight years to reach the Canadian island, Edwards stated. It was covered with moss and barnacles. Supposedly, underneath these was a silver plate bearing Coghlan's name.

Edwards added: "Coghlan once visited a Gypsy fortune teller who told him that he would die at the height of his fame in an American southern city, but that he would have no rest until he returned to the place of his birth, Prince Edward Island. Coghlan often mentioned this strange prediction to his friends. . . ." Edwards adds that Coghlan "was finally buried in the cemetery beside the church where he had been baptized sixty-seven years before—one of the strangest true stories on record."

Is the story really true? What does the evidence say? How believable is Edwards's version of the tale?

Solution

Consider first of all that no one was ever able to locate the supposedly reburied coffin, although Edwards claimed it was in the churchyard cemetery near Coghlan's home. The story's credibility (or believability) suffers further when Edwards states that Coghlan was born on Prince Edward Island. (Did you notice that error?)

Writer Melvin Harris, who investigated this story, states that there are no newspaper accounts reporting the coffin's having arrived at Prince Edward Island, no records of the alleged reburial, nothing. He concluded that "the whole story is a fantasy."

If Coghlan actually told of a fortune teller predicting his death and return home (and that, too, may be pure fiction), it could have provided a basis for the tale. As investigators soon learn, stories like that of the homing coffin grow and are "improved" as they are told and retold, especially by writers who are eager to sell books.

A Note to Teachers

By taking advantage of children's interest in UFOs, ghosts, monsters, and other paranormal topics, *The Magic Detectives* can be used as an illustrative aid for teaching young people valuable skills. All of the book's thirty "cases" help to develop reasoning ability and to promote critical thinking; they also reinforce rational over irrational thought, and science over superstition.

Selected stories can help dramatize particular principles of physics ("Walking on Fire" for heat conductivity, and "Visions of Nostradamus" and "Thoughtography" for certain aspects of optics, for example). Others relate to psychology, biology, archaeology, and additional fields important to an understanding of self and world.

The stories can be used to generate class discussion (as by presenting a case but withholding the solution, so that the class as a group can attempt to solve the mystery). They can also serve as a basis for essays, research (library or field work), experiments or science projects, and the like.

Here are some specific suggestions for assignments:

1. Write an essay explaining the importance of the work done by "magic detectives."
2. With the help of an adult, make a "spirit picture" like those described in chapter eighteen.
3. Report on field work you do on a "haunted" house in your area. Visit the site and try to interview people who tell about the ghost. Examine all claims critically.

4. Read a book on some aspect of the paranormal. Write a critical review a few paragraphs long. State whether or not you recommend the book and why.
5. Discuss with your classmates the ethical difference between the trickery of phony "psychics" and that of stage magicians.
6. Learn a "mind-reading" trick from a book on magic. Perform it for your classmates. Afterward tell them it was just a trick but don't give away the secret.
7. For a science project, put together a display on some aspect of the paranormal.
8. From books on "flying saucers," learn about a UFO mystery that has been solved. Write it up in story/solution form like the cases in this book. Present it to your classmates.
9. Have a member of your class—someone who's good at acting—pretend to be the "reincarnation" of a famous historic figure. Form a group of "investigators" to learn the true details about that figure. "Expose" the false claim on the basis of the actor's inability to correctly answer your questions.
10. With your teacher's help, perform a simple experiment to test whether you and a classmate can read each other's thoughts.

Adapt these or create new assignments appropriate for your students. The idea is to stimulate them to think critically about fanciful claims. And don't be afraid to have fun with them in the process!

Sources Consulted

The Amityville Horror

Anson, Jay. *The Amityville Horror: A True Story* (New York: Bantam Books, 1978).

Lester, Peter. "Beyond the Amityville Hogwash . . ." *People,* September 17, 1979, pp. 90–94.

Moran, Rick, and Peter Jordan. "The Amityville Horror Hoax," *Fate,* May 1978, pp. 43–47.

Morris, Robert L. Review of *The Amityville Horror. The Skeptical Inquirer,* vol. 2, no. 2 (1977–78), pp. 95–102.

Ancient Astronauts

"The Big Picture," *Scientific American,* June 1983, p. 84.

Nickell, Joe. "The Nazca Drawings Revisited: Creation of a Full-Sized Duplicate," in *Science Confronts the Paranormal,* Kendrick Frazier, ed. (Buffalo, N.Y.: Prometheus Books, 1986), pp. 285–292.

Randi, James. *Flim-Flam!: Psychics, ESP, Unicorns, and Other Delusions* (Buffalo, N.Y.: Prometheus Books, 1982), pp. 109–130.

Thiering, Barry, and Edgar Castle. *Some Trust in Chariots* (Toronto: Popular Library, 1972).

Von Däniken, Erich. *Chariots of the Gods?* (New York: Bantam Books, 1971).

Bridey Murphy Lives Again

Brooksmith, Peter, ed. *The Unexplained* (New York: Marshall Cavendish, 1984), vol. 1, pp. 78–80; vol. 2, p. 175.

Gardner, Martin. *Fads & Fallacies in the Name of Science* (New York: Dover Publications, 1957), pp. 315–320.

Wilson, Ian. *All in the Mind* (Garden City, N.Y.: Doubleday & Co., 1982), p. 58.

"Channeling" Spirits

Christopher, Milbourne. *ESP, Seers & Psychics* (New York: Thomas Y. Crowell, 1970).

Keene, M. Lamar (as told to Allen Spraggett). *The Psychic Mafia* (New York: St. Martin's Press, 1976).

Mullholland, John. *Beware Familiar Spirits* (1938; Reprinted, New York: Scribner, 1979).

The Cinder Woman Mystery

Allen, W. S. "Weird Cremation." *True Detective,* December 1951, pp. 42–45, 93–94.

Gadd, Laurence D., and the editors of the World Almanac. *The Second Book of the Strange* (New York: World Almanac Publications, 1981), pp. 35–36.

Nickell, Joe, with John F. Fischer. *Secrets of the Supernatural* (Buffalo, N.Y.: Prometheus Books, 1988), pp. 149–157 (also Appendix, pp. 161–171).

Dark Days

Colby, C. B. "New England's Darkest Day," *Strangely Enough* (abridged) (New York: Scholastic Book Services, 1963), pp. 30–31.

Corliss, William R. *The Unexplained: A Sourcebook of Strange Phenomena* (New York: Bantam, 1976), pp. 236–247.

The Early American Demon

Christopher, Milbourne. *ESP, Seers & Psychics* (New York: Thomas Y. Crowell, 1970), pp. 149–163.

Lowrance, Mason I., Jr. *Increase Mather* (New York: Twayne Publishers, 1974).

Robbins, Rossell Hope. *The Encyclopedia of Witchcraft and Demonology* (New York: Crown Publishers, 1959), pp. 387–391.

The Everywhere Panda

Harré, Rom, and Roger Lamb. "Contagion," in the *Encyclopedic Dictionary of Psychology* (Cambridge, Mass.: MIT Press, 1983), p. 119.

Van Kampen, Hans. "The Case of the Lost Panda," *The Skeptical Inquirer,* vol. 4, no. 1 (Fall 1979), pp. 48–50.

The Geller Effect

Collins, Jim. *The Strange Story of Uri Geller* (Milwaukee, Wisc.: Raintree Children's Books, 1977).

Randi, James. *The Magic of Uri Geller* (New York: Ballantine Books, 1975).

The Ghost Girl

"Apparitions," in Richard Cavendish, ed. *Encyclopedia of the Unexplained* (London: Routledge & Kegan Paul, 1974), pp. 27–37.

Baker, Robert A. Interview by author, January 29, 1980.

Christopher, Milbourne. *ESP, Seers & Psychics* (New York: Thomas Y. Crowell, 1970), pp. 164–173.

The Haunted Stairs

Nickell, Joe, with John F. Fischer. *Secrets of the Supernatural* (Buffalo, N.Y.: Prometheus Books, 1988), pp. 17–27.

Hervey, Sheila. *Some Canadian Ghosts* (Richmond Hill, Ontario: Pocket Books, 1973), pp. 105–115.
Smith, Susy. *Ghosts Around the House* (New York: World, 1970), pp. 38–50.

The Holy Shroud

Browne, Malcolm W. "How Carbon 14 was Used to Fix Date of Shroud," *New York Times,* October 14, 1988.
Nickell, Joe. *Inquest on the Shroud of Turin,* updated edition (Buffalo, N.Y.: Prometheus Books, 1987).
Wilson, Ian. *The Mysterious Shroud,* with photographs by Vernon Miller (New York: Doubleday [Image], 1988).

The Homing Coffin

Colombo, John Robert. *Mysterious Canada* (Toronto: Doubleday Canada, 1988), pp. 66–67.
Edwards, Frank. *Strange World* (New York: Lyle Stuart, 1964), pp. 82–83.
Harris, Melvin. *Investigating the Unexplained* (Buffalo, N.Y.: Prometheus Books, 1986), pp. 191, 194–196.

The Idol of Bel

Asimov, Isaac. *Asimov's Guide to the Bible,* vol. II: The Old Testament (New York: Equinox Books, 1968), pp. 621–622.
"Bel and the Dragon." *New Catholic Encyclopedia.* 1967, vol. 2, pp. 235–36.
Book of Daniel (chapter 14, verses 1–22). *The Revised Standard Version Common Bible.* (New York: William Collins, 1973).
Gibson, Walter. *Secrets of Magic Ancient and Modern* (New York: Grosset & Dunlap, 1967), pp. 16–17.

Lady, the Wonder Horse

Christopher, Milbourne. *ESP, Seers & Psychics* (New York: Thomas Y. Crowell, 1970), pp. 39–54.
Gardner, Martin. *Fads & Fallacies in the Name of Science* (New York: Dover Publications, 1957), pp. 301–302, 352.

The Loch Ness Monster

Gould, Rupert T. *The Loch Ness Monster* (London: Geoffrey Bles, 1934).
"Myth or Monster?" *Time,* November 20, 1972, p. 66.
Welfare, Simon, and John Fairley. *Arthur C. Clarke's Mysterious World.* (New York: A & W Visual Library, 1980), pp. 108–115.

The Mummy's Curse

Cottrell, Leonard. *The Secrets of Tutankhamen's Tomb* (Greenwich, Conn.: New York Graphic Society, 1964).
Evans, Humphrey. "The Curse of the Boy King," in vol. 6 of *The Unexplained* (New York: Marshall Cavendish, 1984), pp. 781–735.
Frazier, Kendrick. "Mummy's Curse Tut-tutted," *The Skeptical Inquirer,* vol. 5, no. 1 (Fall 1980), p. 13.
Perl, Lila. *Mummies, Tombs, and Treasure* (New York: Clarion Books, 1987), pp. 84–95.

Photographing Fairies

Doyle, Arthur Conan. *The Coming of the Fairies* (New York: Samuel Weiser, 1921).
Gardner, Edward L. *Fairies: The Cottingly Photographs and Their Sequel* (London: Theosophical Publishing House, 1966).
Hines, Terence. *Pseudoscience and the Paranormal* (Buffalo, N.Y.: Prometheus Books, 1988), pp. 4–5
Randi, James. *Flim-Flam!: Psychics, ESP, Unicorns, and Other Delusions* (Buffalo, N.Y.: Prometheus Books, 1982), pp. 12–41.

The Reverend Peter Popoff, Healer

Randi, James. *The Faith-Healers* (Buffalo, N.Y.: Prometheus Books, 1987).
Steiner, Robert A. "Exposing the Faith-Healers." *The Skeptical Inquirer,* vol. 11, no. 1 (Fall 1986), pp. 28–31.

Spirit Pictures

Keene, M. Lamar (as told to Allen Spraggett). *The Psychic Mafia* (New York: St. Martin's Press, 1976), pp. 110–111.
Nickell, Joe, with John F. Fischer. *Secrets of the Supernatural* (Buffalo, N.Y.: Prometheus Books, 1988), pp. 47–60.

"Thoughtography"

Eisendrath, D., and Charles Reynolds, "An Amazing Weekend with Ted Serios": Parts I and II. *Popular Photography,* October 1967, pp. 81–87, 131–140, 158.
Randi, James. *Flim-Flam!: Psychics, ESP, Unicorns, and Other Delusions* (New York: Lippincott and Crowell, 1980; reprinted 1988, by Prometheus Books).

Tracking "Bigfoot"

Bord, Janet and Colin. *The Bigfoot Casebook* (Harrisburg, Pa.: Stackpole Books, 1982).
Cohen, Daniel. *The Encyclopedia of Monsters* (New York: Dodd, Mead & Co., 1982), pp. 3–37.
Dennett, Michael R. "Bigfoot Jokester Reveals Punchline—Finally," *The Skeptical Inquirer* vol. 7, no. 1 (Fall 1982), pp. 8–9.

The Tragic UFO Chase

Gardner, Martin. *Fads & Fallacies in the Name of Science* (New York: Dover, 1957), pp. 57–59.

Klass, Philip J. *UFOs Explained* (New York: Vintage Books, 1976; reprinted 1989, by Prometheus Books), pp. 43–46.

Ruppelt, Edward J. *The Report on Unidentified Flying Objects* (New York: Ace Books, 1956), pp. 46–56.

Sachs, Margaret. *The UFO Encyclopedia* (New York: Perigee Books, 1980), pp. 125–126; illus. of Skyhook balloon, p. 294.

Story, Ronald D., ed. "Mantell incident," *The Encyclopedia of UFO's* (Garden City, N.Y.: Doubleday, 1980), pp. 220–221.

The "Two Will Wests"

Cooke, T. Dickerson. *The Blue Book of Crime: Science of Crime Detection* (Chicago: Institute of Applied Science, 1959), p. 43.

Mitchell, C. A. *The Expert Witness* (New York: D. Appleton, 1923)), pp. 26–27.

Nickell, Joe, with John F. Fischer. *Secrets of the Supernatural* (Buffalo, N.Y.: Prometheus Books, 1988), pp. 75–88.

UFO Creatures

Gurney, Gene and Clare. *Unidentified Flying Objects* (New York: Abelard–Schuman, 1971), pp. 74–75.

Story, Ronald D. *The Encyclopedia of UFOs* (Garden City, N.Y.: Doubleday, 1980).

The UFO Explosion

Ballantine, Michael. "It Came from Outer Space," in Martin Ebon, ed. *The World's Great Unsolved Mysteries* (New York: Signet, 1981), pp. 19–29.

Hines, Terence. *Pseudoscience and the Paranormal* (Buffalo, N.Y.: Prometheus Books, 1988), pp. 192–193.

Oberg, James E. "Tunguska (Russia) event," in Ronald D. Story, ed. *The Encyclopedia of UFOs* (Garden City, N.Y.: Doubleday, 1980), pp. 371–373.
Von Däniken, Erich. *Chariots of the Gods?* (New York: Bantam Books, 1971), pp. 122–125.

The Vanished Tanker

Jordan, Kent. "Bermuda Triangle Mystery," in Martin Ebon, ed., *The World's Great Unsolved Mysteries* (New York: Signet, 1981), pp. 50–57.
Kusche, Lawrence David. *The Bermuda Triangle Mystery—Solved.* (New York: Warner, 1975), pp. 206–216, illus. pp. 166–167; reprinted, 1986 by Prometheus Books, Buffalo, N.Y.
Winer, Richard. *The Devil's Triangle* (New York: Bantam, 1974), pp. 130–138.

The Vanishing Olivers

Bierce, Ambrose. "Mysterious Disappearances," in *Can Such Things Be?* (1893; reprinted, New York: Albert & Charles Boni, 1924), pp. 421–424.
Edwards, Frank. *Strangest of All* (New York: Signet, 1962), pp. 102–103.
Nickell, Joe, with John F. Fischer. *Secrets of the Supernatural* (Buffalo, N.Y.: Prometheus Books, 1988), pp. 61–73.

The Visions of Nostradamus

Gibson, Walter. "The Visions of Nostradamus," in *Secrets of Magic Ancient and Modern* (New York: Grosset & Dunlap, 1967), pp. 34–40.
Rachleff, Owen. *The Occult Conceit* (Chicago: Cowles, 1971), pp. 138–139.
Randi, James. "Nostradamus: the Prophet for All Seasons," *The Skeptical Inquirer* vol. 7, no. 1 (Fall 1982) pp. 30–37.

Walking on Fire

Gibson, Walter. *Secrets of Magic Ancient and Modern* (New York: Grosset & Dunlap, 1967), pp. 92–94.

Liekind, Bernard J., and William T. McCarthy. "An Investigation of Firewalking," *The Skeptical Inquirer,* vol. 10, no. 1 (Fall 1985), pp. 23–34.